T0166535

COFFEE-TO-GO SHORT-SHORT STORY SERIES

BARRY SILESKY

# ONE THING THAT CAN SAVE US

COFFEE HOUSE PRESS :: MINNEAPOLIS

The author thanks the following publications that first printed some of these and their variations: *Asylum*, *Black Ice*, *Boulevard*, *Central Park*, *Exquisite Corpse*, *Fiction*, *New American Writing*, *The Prose Poem*, *Texture*, *Trafika*, *Wire*, and *Witness*. "Trophy," "Elegant Dining. . . ," "Love," "Squirrels," and "Pastoral" were heard on National Public Radio's "Sound of Writing," selected by the Syndicated Fiction Project.

The publishers would like to thank the following funders for assistance that helped make this book possible: Dayton Hudson Foundation on behalf of Dayton's and Target Stores; The National Endowment for the Arts, a federal agency; The Lannan Foundation; The Andrew W. Mellon Foundation; Star Tribune/Cowles Media Company; The McKnight Foundation; the Minnesota State Arts Board, and Lila Wallace–Reader's Digest Fund.

Coffee House Press books are available to the trade through our primary distributor, Consortium Book Sales & Distribution, 1045 Westgate Drive, Saint Paul, MN 55114. For personal orders, catalogs or other information, write to:

Coffee House Press
27 North Fourth Street, Suite 400, Minneapolis, MN 55401

Library of Congress Cataloging-in-Publication Data
Silesky, Barry, 1949–
    One thing that can save us / Barry Silesky.
        p.    cm.
      ISBN 1-56689-020-9
      I. Title.
    PS3569.I42I4O54  1994                            93-23691
    813' .54—dc20                                          CIP

10  9  8  7  6  5  4  3  2  1

Printed in Canada

For Sharon, Jesse, and Seth, and
everyone who's been there

# CONTENTS

# SEEK

*for G.B.*

As IN the next plank to continue this oak floor, more
than half-laid but already three days, twice what we
planned. Of course the nailer broke in the heat, and the
storm that finally cooled us filled the basement with a
foot of water, drowning the water heater. Dim and
crowded, the apartment back in the city doesn't look
so bad. If it leaks, it's the landlord's problem and the
rent's so low everyone calls it a gem. We all hear about
those deals, but when *you're* looking, no one wants
children, and your breath's so obviously foreign . . .

With the canoe stacked up on the rocks, it looked
like a night in the desert—food, blankets washed
downstream, adventure gone too real. Hard to believe
we ever wanted it. Then the day's last tour guide
pulled us out in his raft, and when we went back to
salvage the remains, the picnic on the beach made the
losses worth it. But that was years ago. The passport's
expired and the children are coming soon. There's no
way we'll finish the floor in time, and when we do,
that post I put in the middle to hold up the second
floor ruins everything again. We remind ourselves we
could always move, though we both know when we
do, it's permanent: if not the post, a basement full of
water, bad weather, no raft to pull us out.

*

Or a place to sit. Quiet. To hear the breeze ruffling the
oaks, and that bird whistle until it's familiar again, the
name coming back—finch? grosbeak?—that squirrel

percussing, distant, then still. And still, the hammering goes on: drill, nail, saw, driving them off. The floor will be done, and worth it. If only I can imagine. But the temperature keeps rising, a sponge sucking up what space is left, then wringing out the pool that laps against muscle, step, filling the space between image and motion, the word and the water heater raised out of the flood, the peppers weeded, fertilized, grass cut, the floor finally sanded, done. It's a *phoebe*. And the coffee appears. The day performs its acrobatics. When the hammering finally stops of course I miss it. How can we not finish the job? How can I sit, and simply look? I have to see the moss roses' gaudy primaries to dig in their pale spindles. The last plank shining in order to nail it down.

*

And it's old; an idea before the word, if there's any: going after: whatever's alive: quark, up, strange, names for the particle's bounce, guessed by math, space, motion: no one's seen. Then a thread waves in liquid: there's green, there's blue: there's eye tracing light: and a screen in the wound gray mulch recording by spark, by thread. And names: snow gone with Grandma; and Grandpa, married sixty years, backs into the dark. Nothing to do with will, idea: the eaten moon circling, record rain, the Dark Continent lighting its revolution. Before it's done, the snow's gone, and there are children: words nothing compared to the tiny hands, breath, brain's invention. And yet, their words: to come in another snow, long after the grandpa they'll know only by words. Whatever they seek, waiting to be invented: color, reason, motion: as they wait. To drool over the floor: to name it: to bury it: to

# THE HUNTER

THE TRAIL was so clear it's a surprise to find the oaks fallen across it, brown leaves and brush crowding it out, in places gone back completely to the woods' floor. But they know it—the ones who made it for years, and keep it; the ones he's heard skittering through leaves, the ones half fur, half metal, thick stump of limb carved to their weapons. He's glimpsed them from time to time—a swatch of gray, brown, a blotch of orange, heard them crashing through trees. They've seen him too, at a distance, the barricades collected about their dens, the electric drone flickering against the night, the prey strung up in the yard—the one who came up the drive to collect the beautiful young shepherd that strayed, then took it back and leashed it to the wrecked car.

Wind rattles the trees and he reminds himself that this is his home. He plows into the bare brush, watches for the worn line that threads through the copse of white pine. Five shots crack off and a flurry of crow convenes, croaks off into the swamp. The cold fingers of skin tell him this is older than he can dream: the one who took that dog raped his own daughter and now he's plowing down the last hill, his murmur the language passing instructions at the local bar, the high school, the gas station, down the back roads from town, between oaks, aiming its polished sights.

\*

The natives come down to the water, watch the new bird stumble among the reeds: a duck? Too large.

goose? crane? They've seen such things before; in fact, they've been hunting them for years. But that tilt of the head, the dark plumage—the child points in her pink sweater, but it doesn't look up. With the second beer half-drained it can finally speak, and the bartender admits it's his first day too, the quiet grandparents that they're strangers. So he's not completely alone; he can tell the stories—the year he left the city, the fox on the roof, five feet of snow . . . That house still stands and the neighbors smile when he visits. The camp's this way, they tell him, and there's always room as long as he brings his own clothes. After all, it is hunting season and the migration has started. He pecks around nervously at first, but when the organ begins, he sits back.

*

On the way to town he stops at the spring by the river to get pure water: more than he needs, but this way he can ignore the smallness of the room, the alarm going off to the landlord's scowl. Though no radio station can change the flies' endless conversation, this is what he wanted. The children paying the rent at the other end of the phone never hang up. He had to get away. It's just that these extremes are so hard to live with. Either the roof's leaking or a garbage truck's coming right through the wall. Maybe this time he just won't answer. But that's impossible too. It's all so private, even the geese sailing over the swamp, the sun surprising the clouds are no help. They're all going south. The real work's waiting there, and it's closer than he can admit. Already it's almost dark, and the refrigerator's empty. The deer hiding in the woods are going to stay.

# A DECK

I'M BUILDING a new one, and the old cuts fit the edges exactly, square and triangle, angles around the posts, two levels, a view apart from the swamp woods. Clear, green, flute of the crane: I knew why I came here then: something to stand on: measure, cut, nail, and when it doesn't fit, make it. Again. Of course it didn't last. The truck wouldn't start, the saw wouldn't, bad work or none, whiskey and guns, the woman fled to the coast.

This time the planks are solid, two-by instead of flimsy one-inch, "pressure treated," poison forced in to keep against the rot: hang the work clothes apart, scrub clean, try not to breathe the dust, keep the children away. They giggle and spit as the saw whines, the wood's nailed down. The fit's less sharp, the front half an inch off square, the beveled cedar skirt rough at the corners; but this is vacation: bees thick in the pine shrub, sirens, smoke, steel, the infant cries out of sight. So the stair riser's off line. Do it again, the voice says, and she's right. Except the eyes have forgotten. Bills pile the counter. Summer's running out.

*

Then how about a new diet? Another degree? A job with a future? The luxury of this exercise clarifies: pictures mounted, bright against the album's black background: a dip in the river, a glass of wine, the children's delighted cry rolling over the floor. The family smiles for the shot. The formula shuffles in a bare room, constellations wheeling around corners, walls, filling the pages with their masks: the axe hung on the wall, a can of paint, a broken lawnmower. Mice eating the tomatoes. But they leave us a share. We stand on the deck.

*

It's going to last, though the cries go on, the car needs new plugs, again, the bearings shake down the road, again, tires worn, we're out of milk. We need locks, fence to keep our cattle in: a joke, but this morning those babies squirmed over the floor, chewed up a book while I finished nailing. This time we'll pay extra for platinum to start the engine all the way to spring. Pour that extra footing, make sure the front span won't sag. They'll turn into children, sit up square, stare us down. Rise to run through the door. So far the jobs have brought in enough, but for how long? Hard to picture that house when we're gone, shrinking even as the temperature falls, as they cry for dinner, learn their names. Then speak:

*

A stitch in time, make it new, don't put off: a rug for the bedroom floor, vcr, computer, camper, trip to Alaska with the money we get when we sell this house: another summer. The first time we had it listed, an offer came in a month. Too low, you said. Now babies flood the corners, push away the list of repairs collecting across an ocean. When we go back again, we try the radio, write letters, wait for the call: a deerfly bites a face, another ship blown in the gulf. We're hostage: who's running for president, anyway, who thinks it can help?

Maybe we'll get a sitter for the weekend. You swore we've won the lottery: this hunger's supposed to be done. All the way up the coast, the scenery's so gorgeous we won't mind the squirm and howl, work undone, walls, trees, river gone with that deck. Croissants *are* better in Paris. Spectacular, the August glacier on the Brooks Range. The hero must have arrived.

# BEES

HUM THEIR white noise below the jays, breath floating over the ground, gathering against invaders. Soon enough the vandals erase the last weekend. They don't know they've already driven us back, but we got off the rock the rapids hung us on, and the roof hasn't leaked. So what have we lost? A few strands of hair? A chance to win the lottery? Every night they announce the winners, and I've never known one . . . my aunt though! Twenty-five words got her a car and income for life. She signed to never tell the famous rhyme, and the checks keep coming. They keep remodeling their house. Then order a new one—acres on the outskirts and if the relatives don't like it, she doesn't have to talk to 'em. It was another generation. So who's crazy? Tomorrow we'll bury the last vines, and the bees will gather again. They don't know it's the last day. We swear we'll be back.

*

Hand still swollen from yesterday's sting, what is that to the rock 'n' roll deejay at the state fair? They're eating corn by the ton while shoemakers apply for quotas: no protection, the president says, nothing we don't know. So I button up my flannel, denim, lace up the boots and head into the dark. I'm getting rid of the hive—cool, black, flashlight and foolproof spray: sure as the chainsaw sliding through oak like butter. An hour cutting and hauling, and my clothes were soaked with the work. So long away from it, I'll be lucky to stand up and walk tomorrow. I point the spray and fire. This isn't Cape Town, not even frost killing the peppers. One sad bee curls out of the hole then falls back. Dick calls the last time before he goes to China. Sharon wants to play. So much news it's hard to know where to stack the branches. When I check the hives tomorrow, they'll be gone and probably the swelling too. If we can get to Hong Kong, we promise to visit. The bees are everywhere.

*

This morning I take a walk in the mist: fall again, two weeks early, and a handful of bees slips out of the hole in the woods. A leaf, a clump of bark must have saved them from last night's attack. Or I hit the wrong spot. I see them hover near each other, one go back, one take off; another pair, a brief conversation then different directions. They don't know I'm watching. They don't care. Their defense is so local they'd never have bothered if I hadn't been stomping over their door, cutting wood. If Margaret hadn't called to invite us, we could be alone, the last of a race fogged in the island. If Laura hadn't left, Sharon could be rich, the house finished. The swelling's almost gone, and we're going up north this morning to visit the grandparents. It's the biggest news of the day there. We'll have lunch, and again Grandma will forget who we are, where we've come from, Grandpa have still less to say. The hive by the garden's quiet now. This trip's a duty, some pain in the years called back, in what it tells us is coming. In less than a week, the city. Pesto at Margaret's, a weekend of company, a swim . . . the bees thicken with the coming frost. They say it's because spring was early. I try to step carefully, think of the scar still marking my leg, stumble through the branches.

*

Late afternoon sun finally breaking through: the daily newscast is irresistible. The pine fell backward in spite of the hinge I notched, but it missed the house and lay like it was meant for the yard. Paul laughed at the broken chain brake when he surprised me in town. Sharon's promised to help clean up the branches. The swelling gone, only a sometime itch is left to remember the sting. A fresh pile of logs hauled in, laundry done, a hurricane heads for the Florida coast. Up here we'd never know. Or the voices storming South Africa, the teacher strike pending Chicago. Just beyond the driveway the swamp's ready for geese. Margaret and David are waiting for us. I list the chores. Not dead yet, our old landlord grins whenever we say hello. He piles the mail in our basement. We'll find out soon enough what we left. When the sun disappears into pines there's barely an airplane, a jay's whistle, the white hum of bees we can't see. On the way to dinner, I fasten my seatbelt.

# INTERVIEW

THE LAKE spread out the window, rippling in the wind. Thick carpet, stuffed furniture, the wide desk— of course I love the view. Two men filed in, shook my hand. I sank into the couch facing the chairs. What do I want? The ex-wife gone to the coast, I came back to the city. The woman I rode the train with spent the night beside me. Her lover was another friend. I must belong to this suit. They smile and nod. The ex-wife books flights for an airline. When I stayed at her house I saw her body taut against the moonstruck window, and she spoke to me where I lay. She never came closer. Here's the dime that fell from my pocket while I sat on the couch. I bought a newspaper on the way home. Waiting at the newsstand for the train, I look at the sex magazines. In the back corner of the train, a dark-skinned woman draws the shawl tight around her head, eyes down on the book in her lap. *Warfare Prayers* it's titled. Her lips keep mouthing the words.

# THE BOOK

OF COURSE it doesn't exist. The woman who worked
at the post office in the film had small, perfect breasts
she kept leaning toward us. All that soft focus, how
could he resist? How can I? Tracks vibrate, sound,
light, far behind the next curve. Subject: death. Have
another sip, this stuff works quick. If that one on the
beach would just sit up, let her top slip as she smiles
my way. And then? Children's lunch to make, paint
new door, get papers downtown, don't stop now. The
angel in the film was a chiropractor. Insurance won't
pay off. But then, no need to ever think about sex.
When I had the chance, nerve stalled, the skin gave
up. Then we're driving again, and here's the eastern
range, snow carving blue and another hour. Records
in every library, catalogue numbers, old leather, fine
press paper pastel & primary threads wind through.
Or some incense, chanting, the letter flying to the
doorstep, the message nothing hears on the phone
machine. No need. This is a prayer.

# EXERCISE

THE GUY on tv bangs the guitar, bodies shimmering, jerking to music we can't hear. No matter, the view's the point. Besides, we came for the exercise. A woman, walking down stairs, ass barely covered by a scrap of red. The bull's ready to charge. All over the world, they're in bed this minute. Why else do we heave and pant between grins? No one can afford to drag around extra these days, budget out of control another birthday working too hard. We've got to make it last.

Then let's sing along to what we left, bring a few minutes back: grosbeaks dancing over seeds on snow, breath cracking smoke in the blue. Blonde curling out her jeans as she pulled them up. Already I'm forgetting the frozen pump. Her husband, my wife. Or Camille taking me home to smoke, dark skin humming all night I couldn't believe such luck. She sang blues at the corner bar. In the morning she wanted my car.

I'm not going back.

Then a scent, the last slant of sun amber on a bedspread and the day's gone.

Tall, slender, dark, blond, skin and skin and skin—so what if a plane explodes across the planet? A gas stream we can't see dives into a hole in stars and we all edge toward it. The president won by a landslide; we're in good hands. When the aches get too bad, we buy medicine, plan a vacation. If the home team wins on Sunday, we won't even mind the babies screaming. Even now, she's taking off clothes for him, and she is, and she is. These new diseases require much more care, but that's not going to stop us. This is America. Ask anyone.

# CAFÉ MAGIC

THE TEENAGERS raped in a garage on the other side of town knew those guys. It's not our fault. But where's the gold coin falling out of an ear, the witch dissolving in smoke as we burrow into bed? She deserved to become that mouse, hacked to the pieces she tried to make us. Blue sign in front, steel blues on the radio, this is the town. Sun peeks over coffee, and I can see the brick building I'm supposed to find, blurred faces waiting in a closed room. I'll think of something to say. The war's over. It's spring again. Even if our team doesn't win this summer, I can smell the barbecue you're dreaming, the skin of your hair, grass just mown. We got fresh dirt for this year's garden, hacked out the old dogwood to let in light for the vegetables.

On the office door in back, a poster says "Help!" in cute primaries, a hand emerging from a riot of paper on a desk. Dumb but perfect for this town we ought to live in. The café placemat lists the advantages: kids who can read, figure with the best. Okay, so the booths & tables are nothing but plastic, but it's the only place on this strip not fast food. The school sports teams are champions. New research shows that barbecues lead to cancer. There's a "Hero" sandwich—minute steak on bun with lettuce tomato pickle. There's ham & eggs, fettucine, gyros, baked chicken casserole, burgers galore, you name it. All day long, they serve everything.

# PRESENTS

THE WOMAN crosses the street, draws her collar tight against snow, blond-brown hair falling over the round steel frame of her glasses. Everyone knows she's naked underneath, that the cold doesn't reach. She's coming this way. Steam curls up to frost the café window, so sweet out of the wind. Let's dance a slow one. Carved wood leopards pose over her mantle, smoke of sandalwood, black flowers—we all want to live there. As the evening turns, anything can happen. Is that gray streak on the window or her coat? The guy in the lawn chair strapped to helium had the right idea. Sky going on blue and bluer, so cold gasoline turns jelly, and a whole town stops dead. This background symphony is so romantic, if the waitress is a little snotty we don't listen. Soup thick and spicy, the old music a dream—no one mistakes this for vacation, but your skin in the morning emptied my hand. All the newspapers tell us daylight's finally longer again, we can win the war they've been planning for us. Spruce, white pine, Scotch pine & balsam fir decorate all the houses. None of them are ours, but we're invited. The frozen town's a thousand miles away. You promised you'd get the car washed. That woman wasn't nearly as pretty as she first looked and she just kept walking. Now get that kid out of the room and let me sleep before I break something. The snow's barely a coat, but we'll call this Christmas white.

# DOORBELL

Segmented, hollow, hiding in red, yellow, blue rectangles, solids burrowing into each other: a blanket, expanding. That thick tube in the center of the painting's hardly the largest object, but it's the one reaching out.

Can't you think of something besides sex?

He claimed to have slept with over two hundred women and he's coming to our party. Someone made a sign with the number, and we all laughed. Of course the mortgage is due, ceiling plaster falling downstairs, the home team falling into the cellar. Then how about a little fun? It's hard to remember the details—shell blue sky, air warming outside the window.

He sat drinking coffee at the table. He deals junk and travels; he's delighted to run into us here. We can't prove he's not telling the truth, that those women said no, but we're going to find out. The crowd gathers around the park. This is vacation, what's the hurry? Have another coffee, take that class, you're not too old to dance. Or some sports, tennis for instance, seriously this time, as he is, middle-age champion, before it's too late. We've plotted this for years, everyone's sick of the whining. I've got my own kids too, and not much time before I've got to pick them up, explain the "facts of life." Mix two or three parts sand to one part cement, depending on the weather, and how hard you want it to cure. This new plastic spray foam is great for sealing cracks. Her skin's first curve under cloth. She's sitting right there, let her know you're looking; she likes it when it's discreet.

How soon the cells revolt, and the rent's forced us out before we even blinked. Have a drink at breakfast. The Russian empire's come to an end, now it's those drugs coming up from the south. One little taste can't be that bad. Touch me, here.

When we're finally home and the doorbell rings, it's as if we've been waiting forever. The approach is so clumsy, he gets slapped often enough, but it must be worth it.

The package is no surprise, but then, we haven't opened it.

# SALMON

SHE LOVED to eat. When they begin their famous migration they have no idea. The first winter, pools of water condensed on the plastic we stapled to the rafters too loose for a vapor barrier. We never expected to stay. We hadn't finished hanging the last quarter with Sheetrock. She said it was stupid to let water sit there and pulled the plastic down. The view from her balcony over the bay to the city stopped my breath. She poured another glass of wine before the restaurant. It took three years for the ceiling to sodden and fall. The post she hated that held up the beam in the middle of the downstairs room was my mistake. She likes her new job. She built two stairways solid, one straight to the basement, one to the upstairs with its right turn, two landings. Her brother bought her a new car for her birthday. She says she's gained weight, but I couldn't tell. She liked the way he would come quick, then get hard again and last. The salmon's delicious. The spice rack she built from a shingle pallet hangs next to the stove. I always loved it. She wasn't going to again with him, but she was leaving the next week; how could she resist? The flesh was so moist and tender, the sauce a real surprise. Maybe she talks a little slower. The backdoor she hung fits perfect. I think his name was Tom. It warped and cracked in the weather since she went. The next summer I built the porch it opens to. She thinks this boyfriend might be the one. She's sorry she didn't tell me she was leaving for good, she just didn't know. Hazel eyes quick, shoulders wide, breasts small but full, chestnut hair, waist thin, whole body jerked tight when she came. She still loves to eat. Her bad knee made her quit tennis after she moved. She thought she'd be married again in a year. Her father's nearly blind. She hopes she can still have a baby. The door to the closet she built warped, but it still shuts tight. These Pacific chinook swim hundreds of miles to spawn then die. Aren't we both happier?

# ELEGANT DINING UNDER THE EL

THE SHOW looks good so far, but Cindy just can't get the part right. Can Mike and Jan cover? The conversation's easy, but it's serious. By the time my eggs come, someone else has taken the booth, tea & granola, *Autobiography of a Yogi*. I learned to fold my legs, count breath until walls bled, hear the ringing. I wanted Mary. We kissed in the grass, May humming every cell. Then went home to my wife. We were on the way to the mountain. We loved everyone.

An old friend I never expected met our plane, hauled me to a corner to warn me: someone from the church he quit had taken his new wife's son. If I heard anything, *please* . . . The migrant shack they lived in warmed with fire & talk all night. We knew this was the way to God. At the church they moaned and clapped their own language. The pastor said I'd be rich. That my friends would find the way. We all prayed. Climbed ladders to harvest fruit. The child never appeared.

Hunched in the cold, someone's riding a bike against traffic, someone's gazing in the window, the train squeaks and roars another circle. The new candidates have all come to town. They swear we'll find jobs. That crack dealer's going straight. Just trust me, once. I haven't got a gun. We've got great seats for the circus, a new couch, transmission fixed. We know our vote won't change it, but they're so friendly at the firehouse, the thin punch going neatly through the card makes each choice certain. We picked those peaches years ago. I can feel the orchard at the desert's edge, juice and sweetness spilling from our mouths.

# EL JARDIN

HE FLIPS on the tube in the corner as the waitress brings the menus. The woman wants to watch 5, but this is *his* day off. He goes through the channels, her smile blanks.

"Take this beauty here, a real cream puff," the voice says, and he can't decide. Of course she's beautiful, but everyone knows he's selling junk. Inside a year the used Dodge I bought blew the water pump then transmission. The air-conditioning never worked. He's old enough to know, but it's all right, this lunch takes time. Her voice caught his breath all week. Winter sun butters the floor, he lights a smoke, and it's a new year, they're planning the trip to Mexico. Diet sodas come, she flicks blond across her brow. Hands wrapped behind his head as he slumps back, lean, thin moustache, her eyes say he's cute. One of these nights she just might tell him. Ten years later their kid pulls over a lamp, she's pissed he won't talk, the vacation's ruin. How did she get that weight, his hair so thin, his crude friends—? He gets up to pee, and she grabs the remote to change it, but her finger hangs over the button.

The voice screams, "Both of us in love!" and the man in the close-up looks away. It's past time to leave. It's someone else's vacation anyway. When he gets back, the waitress comes with both our meals, sets them down. His date didn't order. We bend over the plates.

# SQUIRRELS

THE GUITARIST she'd married left for the city. When my wife and I divorced, she moved into the house, close enough to her family that she could leave the baby at times. They live nearly anywhere, travel head-first, all directions. Their tails are rudders in water, parachutes when they jump. They were everywhere that winter, and fat, and she got plenty to freeze, along with some rabbits. They don't hibernate. Most are brown or gray. A few reds or blacks show up each year, but they're always too small to bother. She took out the screen in the window over the kitchen sink, raised the sash a crack to lean the barrel on the sill when she shot. They have excellent sight, in full color. She wanted to be a doctor. She thought she should lose some weight. Her baby screamed at the explosion. She hugged and cooed till the baby calmed, then ran out the door to get what she shot. The meat was tough, tasted something like chicken but darker. We drank the wine I'd brought, hummed with the old music from the stereo upstairs. I was glad to take a second helping. All the meat came from what she got through the window. She said I should learn to go slow, but I only wanted to finish. She said she'd come to the city to visit. She went to medical school, came back to work for the county, but it didn't last. She fought against anti-abortioners, held a gun on tv news. I saw her new boyfriend in town. We'd met before but didn't speak. She never did come to visit. She got out of bed before sunup, left to hunt with her brothers.

# GEORGE WASHINGTON

U-HAULS HOME from their rents, ballpark done for the year, night coming early—this must be his street. His name's right there on the cab license. Without the beard he's grown, half-dyed red, roots growing white, the picture looks years younger, someone else. Of course he knows the answers. "Eat!" he tells the grandson who's "half-Southside, if you know what I mean," pointing to his coiled hair.

He means Africa. He means the truck he invented to drive through the lake, the plastic roof that won't leak, a dozen cities in Europe he's worked in, every state he's seen, more things than you can dream since he came from the war that taught him everything. He can guess anyone's age. Atlanta's set a curfew for kids under seventeen. The two dozen killed by guerillas in El Salvador were on the wrong side. The Boston prostitute raped and stabbed a hundred times was working for crack. He looks right through the grandson. He doesn't ask.

The fast-food burgers fill us. Congealing the gut under old ballplayers retired and dead, they're a long way from what we'd choose, but the kids know this is heaven. He leans closer. He went to Israel last year. His youngest son just got married. In Russia, they want to build a church for the last czar. Plenty of garlic, but not enough meat, beets, cabbage, everyone getting hungry. The new war's brewing half a world away. Two fires, three murders this weekend. Tomorrow we'll drive back east for holiday thanks.

Done with their ice cream, my own kids want to go out and play, but those burgers make it hard to move. They want to know why he sounds so funny. Doesn't eat a thing. Keeps talking.

# THE REST

*"The pure products of America go crazy . . ."* —wcw

SITTING IN leather chairs, oogling the secretary. Just one little nip between appointments. A few more planes, beachfront hotel, haven't I earned the trip to the Bahamas? Sweet ganja, float dem coconut palms on the rippling blue: there we could all live forever. But the plane back's already leaving and we can't miss it. When we get home, the baby dumps lunch, pulls down the bureau and we never left. Okay, let's take a walk on the sun-drenched roof atop the club before it's over. The pool welcomes everyone, just look at that body. We're so lucky to belong. String taut in her pink suit, why not join her? The rest of the place nearly deserted, no one will find me. Leaves of potted lemons catch the sprayed light, the new president promises air we can breathe, better schools, let me put it in just once, just a second, I promise I

But she's half my age, what could I be thinking?

Playing guitar all night next to the woodstove, smoke, kerosene light . . . Tell me what I forgot that sat me here, electricity chewing brains long gone. Scent of juniper and earth, the San Juans, the whole valley spread before us. I sat, and breathed. Hauled water & measured & cut & hammered, banked fire &

Dawn, the garbage picker hit me for change & I looked for something to bash him. A baby to throw through a window, the car to drive through the house. Everyone knows these measures are temporary. Pour coffee, open the newspaper, in a minute the shaking'll stop. I know he's hungry. Every woman is beautiful. Refrigerator's full & waiting. A quick drink would help. They're killing mayors in El Salvador and people are trying to fight back, but the guerillas can't be stopped. Now the old man's choking again. It's your turn to save him.

# HEALTH INSURANCE

Tape up the broken window and keep smiling. It's no joke. Whatever the job I never got, I'm fired. But then, we'll just imagine we can pay. You're so beautiful, surely they'll give us the medicine; we've always lived this way. The woman who hailed my cab leaned over the seat, and I could swear she blew in my hair. When she asked me what I liked, it was time for the next fare. I learned to saw an edge, chisel a hinge plate, hang a door square. If it wasn't quite, it always seemed to close. Beer tastes great with breakfast, and there's finally time to read: the minister who locked his baby in a room three days and didn't feed him taught a lesson we should all know. The kid grew up, wrote books to honor his father. Add a little sex, and we're ready for the next war. Too bad we all thought the home team would win everything; now they're barely out of the cellar, and we can't ignore them. Fortunately it's not our problem. We can slip the check and be gone before anyone even sees.

# HISTORY

WHAT IF we're wrong? It was my turn to make the kids' dinner, the home team can win it all, the war is just as the president says. Just. After all, he's not that old. He went to the best schools, got rich, he must know something. My wife's uncle believes, and if it weren't for the money he sends us, we'd never go out to dinner. Kids here forever, not a minute to think a word in the last months to divorce. We stay at the Central Park apartment he keeps for "business." When the phone rang three A.M. a woman's breathy voice told him he had to come to this party. Now the flu's almost gone and I can plan to get drunk again. Summer *is* coming. Everyone agrees yesterday's peace offer was sham, the bombing must continue. Too bad about the burnt children. Of course we hate the killing, all the money flying out the borders. Children in the suburbs can't sleep. The stomach stalls at tv, lights dive into explosions across the living room, faces twisted with grief. Let me pour another whiskey while the show breaks to the hip-hop beat box. Get our own kids for supper. Your skin was so lush in the bath, maybe we'll have sex again sometime. If the barbarians aren't stopped now, when? With God's help, we're sure to win. If only I'd gone to law school like I was supposed to, it'd be me at that conference table twenty stories up, leaning back in the chair, deciding this expensive question. It isn't tv, some joke, tongue in cheek. My wife's already asleep, and it's past time to be there. Get up early, work, eat. This is history.

# JESSE

*for my son*

ONE WENT CRAZY, waved a chair at his mother, rocked his niece "on the edge of Catatonia." Another robbed banks with his brother, died in the nowhere plains. They say he gave the loot to poor farmers, but we know he kept his share. One ran for president, promised fair prices, justice like music. He rides a limousine, runs late-night talk on tv. I saw the show once, but couldn't resist outer space, flashing lights, another world. If only it were true. Of course I knew the end way before the lawn seed commercial and still stayed up too late watching. Now morning sun pours down the table cold but bright. Please, not this neighborhood; we like to see at a distance. Luckily the guy stinking the subway doesn't vote, and the president swore he'd be kind. Maybe if the new mass murderer had a friend. He was close, the same initial, but in another town. And that bus full of Girl Scouts scrambled over the cliff? The child's plastic lawnmower clatters across the living room.

"No!" he says. "No! No!"

# MARCO'S PARADISE

THE GUY at the bus stop chews his toothpick, walks a circle, steps off the curb to look. Peace treaty signed. Baseball team wins again. No bus in sight. He comes back, walks more. The bright blue and yellow marquee of Marco's Paradise, intricate reds and greens on yellow decorating window and door frames, ask why we're out here instead. Come in! The food's not much, but when did that matter? This is our neighborhood, and we're delighted, or ought to be. The bus *is* coming, bicyclists and whatever desperates running half a step too late to catch it be damned. Salsa rhythms fill the walk until the horns cancel our ears. The notes are clear. When the El shrieks by on its long circle, we don't even hear it.

I read your letter again today, how you're still cooking in the hills up north, tomatoes and peppers are huge, and I want to drink amaretto on your deck, touch your hand. The old lady's pissed all week at the broken window, the stairway half-finished. Russians killed six in the Baltics. Let's stop in, have a beer. Maybe if we wait long enough, something will turn up—your address in Spain, the exact measure for the uncut stair riser, one of those bugs we left in the swamps by your house. They finally turned down that awful music. The war's over, and this is "the new order." When the bus comes and passes, someone else is standing on the corner, sunglasses, cigarette, staring at the window. Mabye he's seen Marco, even knows him. Maybe he's tried the place. Maybe he likes it.

# ANOTHER JOKE

THE KID from the suburbs drove in to get stoned, wound up dead on a sidewalk. Of course I'm worried about money, where the kids are tonight or next week. The Japanese market's the biggest in the world and caving fast. Now that the war's over, they're telling women to pray when their men beat them. It's a friendly country.

In front of the room, tv's selling musical instruments so hard it's got to be a joke. Then the rerun laugh track breaks over the room in case we missed it. I'm not stupid, nobody here is. Upstairs in skin-tights they're stretching, spreading legs so wide we can almost see. Then a week later she can't stand the smell, wants breakfast downtown, car & baby to show her friends. Look at the kid laugh at the end of the show. Grandpa fixed us bananas and milk after the news, took us to the office Saturdays to play with the machines. We made the numbers clatter and hum as if this business were real. They keep coming up the stairs, blond, dark, straight, curled . . .

The old show's over. The home team lost again. "How to keep your job till you're ready to leave," the poster announces. There's the one I want. Then she's gone, and I was wrong again. Dinner's waiting at home. Pick up the kids and get there. It's no joke.

# SHOES

NINETEEN KILLED at the ancient shrine, broken glass all over the alley crumbling to dust, does anyone still believe? Half a world away wool prices are falling like crazy, but nothing's cheaper here. The new drive-ins are take-out only, no one's got time to sit down. Luckily we can still afford the foam spray to stop the windows' leaking. The stuff will shrink to nothing if we don't wrestle the ladder between wires to trim and paint it, but there's sure to be a few days left before it snows. That woman walked straight toward me. I remember the scent. The wires are insulated so it's safe to climb as long as the ladder's steady. She sits nearby, talks to another, clearly business. Behind the counter they put out appetizers. Have a hot dog. Not too healthy, but they won't kill me. All night cleaning the house and it's a mess again. What's her name? She leans over to make a point, shirt open to the skin's first swell. The rain leaks through the hole I wore in the sole of the old shoe the salesman swore would last. Looking for a new brand, I got the same ones again. A party's always a good idea no matter what we believe. Thirteen murdered right here last weekend. Such a beautiful day, what about that ride we were going to take? When I rise to walk to the counter, my foot catches the table, cup & saucer smash on the floor. Everyone stares. The shoes fit exactly.

# MOUNT PLEASANT

ISN'T IT? Warm light, clack of plate, silver & hotel coffee hot & live. Asleep, there were days of negotiations, the famous speaker outraged our offer was so cheap: was I crazy? I was so sorry, what could I have thought? Then *he* was sorry, hugged and kissed me, said he'd see me tomorrow and speak. He's so famously gay I'm still a little nervous—what if he wants to sleep with me? The cop came up from behind in a brightly lit room. I was standing with a few other friends and family. He touched my arm, sweat broke out in a hiss of breath. He wasn't one of the tough city types, more middle-aged, sandy white hair, brown uniform. He was going to arrest me. I could have run, got away. I was cold. I curled deeper into the blanket around me. The Yucatan beach where we got it was cloudy, cool, and we were the only ones there when the peddlar came over the sand. It was ten years ago. We flew home in the afternoon. I haven't left the country since.

Now the war's over & the whole city slowed for the parade celebrating the victory. The home team won again. The recession's "bottomed out." Crabapple trees full blossom, rock 'n' roll lights the new roof carpenters are putting in across the street. In the drive on this side, our children hunt ants. They want to squash them with their hands, eat them. They've seen enough inside the synagogue, heard the ancient chants. A boy's coming of age, reciting a language trying to live. News reports ten times more millionaires now than ten years ago. Foreigners starving in mountains across the world. One child thinks he wants to go back in. Maybe I can take him. Maybe the drive to this town wasn't too long and lunch is coming soon. There isn't a real mountain in the whole state, but those children don't care. The temperature rose all night. The woman yelling at my car the night before was a whore, her breasts spilling wonderfully toward the window, practiced, and desperate.

# LOVE

WHOSE PAINTING is that hand, cut off at the finger, face twisted on a knuckle? Or the one with a phone, a book, some abstract heart half-wound by wire? The painter cut off his fingertip to impress a lover, another jumped off a train for a bar, and a woman waits half the night for him to call. This is supposed to be love. The crooked dictator actually in jail, across the ocean they celebrate the end of the old regime. After frozen December, we've got spring in January, any second, tulips and crocuses rise.

So the toilet sits in the bathtub, a hairline crack at the bottom of the water tank, screws too rusted to separate it for remounting. The valve to the supply pipe replaced too late, the drip soaked through the floor to fall through the neighbors' ceiling. Not much to patch, but the tile on half the floor came up, the toilet seal broke and leaked. We can't use it. Mortgage car insurance taxes electric day care telephone gas fender for the car I hit last fall, all due the next two weeks on part-time wages. Bob at the hardware store says this guy'll fix it up right. The price, if we can get him? It doesn't add up. The Khmer Rouge are killing again, taking cities, lines in Poland stretch out with barely a sausage, a loaf of bread at the end. Tonight's dream opens on the father who left before I knew, grinning across the barbecue. Thousands celebrate the opened border, friends, family everywhere, and I want to tell them the movie last night was great, it's wonderful to see them at last, but I've never heard this language. If we can get through the month, the rest of

the year, maybe a new job to pay it will come. Stuffed
with pizza and wine, nobody here's dying this week.
The man who maimed himself for love shot through
paint cans to spatter the colors on plywood, then cut
and framed the squares to hang in galleries. Dad grins
right through me, never says a thing. Kiss me. Here.
Those paintings are pure invention.

*

A living room, one or two others, and the man who's
famous. Someone tells him it's time, hands him the
rubber finger of flesh he ties around his head. It's a
long cock, fit over his nose, and the room is suddenly
huge, a gym filling with people as we stand at the foot
of the stage. He's going to speak, and we've all come
to listen, cheer his words, so proud he knows us, he
must be my father.

Or the next night we're talking in a small room, two
or three of us, news from Europe, the president's lying
again, I should go to Central America. He's shaved the
beard he's had for years, only a little white stubble on
his chin, and when I suddenly notice, he smiles that
dry whimsey everyone knows him for. I stroke my
own beard, thinking, it must be time.

*

Across the lounge, the blonde's face says something's
wrong. This isn't a painting. The man across the small
table leans his chin on his palm and listens. He's a few
years older, and he's going to fix it: Yes, she smiles
faintly, then wider, sips her water, leans back and
nods. She will have that dinner, that drink, come
home with him, let him take off her—

Now she laughs aloud. The room buzzes with the crowd coming at the end of work. Tonight she's beautiful. He grins at a younger man passing, who stops and talks. Someone across the room waves. Someone else takes down the string and cone to open the stairs they painted. Then he's gone to another room, and she's not beautiful—relieved and blank as the factory table, a handful of scars on her face. She looks around, glances up at the light, faces crossing the stair landing. Do I know her? How long will it be and what's for dinner anyway? Lost in the rush hour of another city, no husband's found her. I'm hours late again.

# OCCASIONAL MUSIC

THE OLD GUY stinks again, why doesn't someone tell him? He's sitting there crying in a chair, what am I supposed to say? Then a month later he's back like it never happened. No one broke into the car, ripped up the ignition. It was her fault all the time. The check really is in the mail. When it comes, the kids still hate us, though they've learned to keep their mouths shut, at least while we're in earshot. She was beautiful, the way her skin rose in my hand. I know you understand the problem. The garbage collectors in that Caribbean country are on strike, or is it Kenya, the post office in Liberia? With the long war over, we're half lost. She invited you under her shirt, and you thought it was always this way. The piano tinkling faintly downstairs proves you're not alone, and the snow coating the empty seats in the picture makes the neighborhood look so inviting. Of course the El train outside the window derails. Have a beer, watch some tv. That man who's playing could be you. The notes are getting clearer, though they're less and less like any tune. Come along for a while, you can hum under the skin. When the rash breaks out there's no need to hold back the tears. You're right at home.

# PASTORAL

*for Dan & Gina*

THE RABBITS used to be pets before they got too fat for the hutch and got away. Now they've eaten the straw flowers we planted to dirt, and they won't leave. Why should they? Peppers coming back from the late frost, tomatoes growing, strawberries ripe . . . But the chicken's still loose from the coop. The old rooster stays close as if to protect her—or to get his piece, if he still can. They both hang near the high weeds they slip into whenever we try to come near. Another perfect day, the pale unbroken sheet of blue sealing us in: the right breeze, bird song, herd of cattle dappling the brown hill. We're supposed to get the chicken back in. It's not ours, this well-made corner—house, two sheds, gardens and chickens, trampoline, twin decks, flowers, grass—left to us a week by friends. We can't let them down.

The woman across the street calls her husband, and when he answers the tone cuts: don't bother me now, it's not my problem. A sheep bleats in the next pasture. Okay, she says, but her voice says it's not. The sheep's plaint rises, a plane drones closer, a truck coughs up the drive. The babies are up from their nap, and the kitchen needs cleaning. I'm beginning to hate you, strutting through this house like I'm supposed to be your maid. It's a hundred degrees back home, you're lucky to be here. The fat guard down the road didn't like his job and shot a half-dozen people he was supposed to protect. It could have been anyone. Soon enough it gets dark. The woman next door says she'll help us hunt the chicken. She wants to use the rooster to keep out something. Her man sold drugs and beat her before he got busted, and now more guys come, crank up the stereo. Can she really help? We've got to get that chicken. The babies are screaming. He ought to be shot. Why can't we stay forever?

# PRACTICAL OCCULT

WORDS for the mail? Sing it backward. Pink and purple flowers tie-dyed on her t-shirt are no accident. It's not going to rain. Why doesn't her husband understand his raise was certain? The cat stalled before it raced by, the black-haired woman touched his hand. She drapes her long braid across her chest and down to her hip. The younger woman she talks to brings her hands together next to the book. Fingers arched at rest on each other, thumbs touching, she knows those men can't be trusted. Four-year-old mauled in pit bull attack. Gubernatorial candidate propositions teenagers. The children's Halloween ghost sheets make them impossible to recognize. Across the street, amnesty classes, a flag rippling in the breeze. What could be more beautiful?

The one with the braid grimaces, lace slip peeking from the pastel skirt.

"He didn't have to sleep with her," she says.

Tomorrow it rains again. The younger woman opens the book, reads instructions. The other nods. Every table is filled. The older woman smiles as they rise to leave.

A voice says, "I don't know what love is, but can I have some sugar?"

The older woman nods again, explains her way home. In the back room, leaves rise and green. A truck drives into a living room.

# OKTOBERFEST

THIS MORNING every capital's in the sixties. Rain in Amsterdam, Brussels partly cloudy. In London, the fake café around the corner from the West End house where we stayed served coffee I loved each morning. We rented bikes, watched a play, rode up the Thames to a castle. Ten years, and those names must be written somewhere. Here's a shilling from the week we spent, a peso from another in Mérida. Everything costs so much more, who can keep up? Might as well sit here and read the paper; that way, they say, we can learn where we are. Tourist stabbed in subway. Soldiers slaughtered and ate most of the animals in the zoo of another country. The Central Park jogger who was raped and beaten pulled herself back from nothing by a lifetime of looking one way. Now Robin's going to Germany, and the two countries that've been all our lives are gone into one. Just don't look around too fast. It's evening there, buildings wave in the mind's breeze, turn into clowns, the mouth of each doorway inviting us in on the joke: have some food, drink, the best beer in the world. Sleepless nights, worry the mortgage due, invading mice on their way from the apartment downstairs—might as well have another. In a few hours the real party begins, everyone so glad to meet you, it might as well be for you. Then it is. The children are finally in school. No one we know has been sent to the new war. Time to get some exercise, watch the women pass, breasts outlined under thin cloth. In a month summer's long gone, clothes thick over everyone who's not inside.

Then keep your eyes open. The guy standing by the rocks at the shore, lean, white-haired, is running his own beer stand. Three guys waiting to tee off at the course on the other side of the fence come over, and they all grin. I haven't even got pockets, let alone money, but I've run far enough. I want one.

# PARIS

SHE'S COMING up the stairs, the kitchen floor's a mess, where's that gun? One twitch and I'm safe for good. But wait: no one here's missing lunch. The woman who murdered her baby daughter is going to jail for life, the man who raped and killed another child was sentenced to death. What more do we want of the morning? Another drunk's chronicle of his trip west isn't ours. "The mountains go papier-mâché" by afternoon he said, but it was forty years ago. These children need a car to go fast, candy, a gun, that present in the box announcing the impossible future of next week's birthday. They mean it, and it's wrong to think it's easy. More snow coming and I still haven't caulked the windows, sent the petition to save the dolphins, stopped the war in El Salvador, Peru, the alley across the street. It's warm in Mérida, thick with the smell of dust, oil, cilantro and pepper, and we were going this year. Or a house in the Paris suburbs—friends want to trade it next summer for ours. But those kids won't eat the rice you cooked. I know the azaleas will open in April, and it's someone else's murder. We won't be there to see it, though the papers give more details than we need. Send me a picture along with the map, I want to see if he's still right about those cliffs. She's banging the door to remind me they need tending. They're animals. They're our children.

# BULLETIN BOARD

CROUCHED on her knees, black hair curled and wound past her waist, red baseball cap backward on her head, she leans forward and talks and talks and talks.

"Why didn't he just ask, Why didn't he tell her, Why didn't he—"

Maybe tomorrow he'll mow the lawn one last time, fix the broken windowsill. Maybe the kids won't piss in their pants.

Wood beams hang suspended in a hub from the darkened ceiling, to remind us what holds it up, or what used to. Here they're pure decoration, the kids' blots on paper and rug grown huge and expensive. Another old idea, arranged to seem modern—the style punctuating the spaces that gather us.

On the wall across the lounge, a neon bulletin board spells out news: "William Tell was Swiss" and "Tad vows revenge after he rescues Dixie from mental institution."

In the dim light, the woman keeps talking beautifully. Her size is 7, she swears she'd love anything he'd buy—an ice cream bar, a flower.

"Guerillas demand more. Two Americans killed to make their point."

Then black lace underwear. Earrings. Gold. I could watch for hours. Outside it must be getting dark but there isn't a window anywhere. The rebels won't be ignored.

# SNOW

LEAVES about to blood, gold, not too hot, anyone could stare forever. Well, a minute or two. Any day the black stack out the roof of the building across the alley belches, and the windows shut. Time to break out the snow shovel. Let's hope the trap worked, the mice the tenants found in their pantry are dead. Last week we had our own, slipping along the gas pipe through the wall behind the stove. I sealed it off, but the mouse was only wounded. I've got to find the crack they slip into before the weather turns and they come in earnest, take over the house. Four years later we've finally cleaned up the storeroom, but the insulation I tried to staple in the rafters is falling. Still, the kids actually sleep most nights, play by themselves for hours. Well, half an hour. They love *The Wizard of Oz*. Just turn the switch. The war's over. Of course a new one's just starting but that desert's half a planet away, and we're finally too old to go. This is the success we all dream. Buy a new coat. Get this other one altered to fit. Tonight, the ball game, the team really coming on the last half of the season. If the day's not so great, try some frozen yogurt—not fattening and so tasty. When it does snow no one's ready.

# THANKSGIVING

THE RESTAURANT´s empty, coffee black and fresh. The leaky gas valve on the heater outside the kids' bedroom's fixed, and no fire. The check didn't bounce. As the plane took off the kids stared out the window, dumb at the vanishing lights. The pay for the last job wasn't enough, but it finally came in the mail. In the car by the frozen lake, my first girlfriend let me touch her breast while my mother and sister cooked at home. The children played with the toy garage Grandma bought them, and we could read the paper, talk about news. It snowed six inches, so we could build a snowman on top of the hill above the lake across the street from Mother's apartment. The boys slogged and rolled and threw snow in the air. At first I thought I was supposed to apologize, not touch her where she let me. "Uproarious!" "Triumphant!" "Great Fun!" the comedy's ad plastered to the door in this café's entry announces. Then she let me more. If the soup's a little watery, the bread's fresh. When Jesse wakes from his nap he likes to lie in my lap while I hold him. The woman who's car I hit hasn't called back for money. I fixed the sill that fell out of the downstairs window. That summer the house was empty mornings, and she came to my bed. They've finally grown out of the diapers that stunk up the house. The tire went flat on the way to dinner with the whole family in the car, but I got it changed in the traffic before the rain. I rode my bike through the clear winter streets to work. When I pushed the mop over the kitchen floor, my back strained, spasmed three days, but healed so well I don't even think of it. Her hand on my skin in the dark. After the kids were asleep I could finally eat, though the turkey was nothing like what I remember. The wet smell of her sex. No one knows where I am.

# SACRIFICE

A BUNCH of kids bounce about machines, balls, sticks of flesh, talk about "sacrifice": if the colonel has to die in the sand, he says he will, and gladly. The young guy leaning on the jeep, hand on pistol, is proud to be there. He's got to believe. We all do. Too bad the car's fender was caved in by that foreign asshole, of course he's got no insurance. Now that the season's over and the last beer bottles are gone from the lawn, the crisp aroma of burning freshens the air. A little pain, sweat, skip dinner, work late again. The bonus is in the mail. The war's finally over.

But that was last year, the other side of town, across the border. Truth is, we haven't been there, nobody has, all we've got are reports. The new café's a little pricey though the salmon's delicious. The home team's plotting the trades sure to lead them back up. The drinks at that bar are famous. Halfway through the second, every woman is beautiful. When she doesn't ask you over, you can still sell real estate, go to law school, like you were supposed to. The beach on that distant coast has plenty of space, and the blonde in the skintight suit is looking your way. You may not be fluent, but the language is music. The desert's so hot we can't imagine.

# PARADISE

BLUE SKY pours over the mail. Rock 'n' roll shrieks through the windows from the building next door. A mall's coming to the next block—health club, parking, boutiques to raise the neighborhood prices still more. We moved here just in time. In the alley below, scavengers clatter yesterday's beer cans. The mortgage payment's late again. The man in the picture sucks at her nipple, his finger along the pink ridge of her sex. The neighbors finally boarded up the gangway next to their garage where the drinkers sneak off to piss. Bronze skin, black hair, long red nails, rings on each finger, she holds his cock hard against her belly. At least this summer was cool and kept down the stench, but the tenants downstairs complain, and who can blame them. The kids are still down for their nap and should be for at least another half-hour. On the next page, his tongue reaches toward the wet flush his fingers hold open. The car needs a tune-up, but after sixty thousand miles, it's still lurching along. The woman who traded her daughter for coke was sentenced to jail. So warm and clear, mid-September, I actually look forward to going to work. The picture can't give us the smell, or the feel, but I know. The new South African president promises to end the state of siege. Our own is sending more troops against the coke dealers. I can almost hear her ragged breath. He says we can get them. Now.

# MOVIE FOR VACATION

SOMEONE falls in love. A bank is robbed. Two more cops shot across town. They make a tow zone in front of the house to clear the curb for the movie, so we've got to move.

Honolulu! That's it!

No, Paris!

No, Tangier!

Except the Arabs have taken over, women veiled, no kif. The canyon at the edge of the Utah desert we visited could have been the moon, brown-gray peaks written on blue, beating in waves to the acid we danced. Or the beach on the Pacific, wrapped in morning fog. She loved sex from behind, in stairwells, any place different. Dan was a priest, his shirt a flag he waved as he stood on a rock in the blue.

The new ticks in the woods where we lived carry a disease named for a town in her home state. They're so small we could barely see them. Maybe we'll go back, visit those woods. She left in winter. The grass in the yard here needs cutting, and somebody keeps leaving dog shit on the tree lawn. At least nobody clipped the tulips this year.

When the camera starts rolling, we don't actually see the action, but we don't have to. Grapes thicken on the vine in the yard. Blond brushes skin. One hair curls under her nipple. Though pigeons and sparrows get all the grapes the squirrels leave, we get to see them. Isn't he lucky? Aren't we? No picture can begin to get the scope, but I can look at them for hours. Sun comes out for the barbecue. Behind the walls is another story, but with all the renovation the neighborhood must be improving. Let down a strap, maybe we can get a part in the excitement. When he leaves her for good, it's too bad, though no one's surprised. If the machines next door don't stop that racket I will. An hour after dark they call it a "wrap," and everyone cheers. Next month the street is everywhere.

# TROPHY

THE BALL was solid black, middle and third finger holes spread too far, but I could hold it. It was Dad's. Of course he wouldn't let me use it. I was learning. Toe at the second dot from the right, four steps to the line, just let it down to the diamond on the board straight ahead, bring the whole hand up to the side. I knew in three feet if the curl would trace the right path. Once in a while it did. I always hit something. I was "respectable." When I lit the grass on the bank next to our house, I put it out before the fire department got there. I could catch every football I could reach, was quick enough to get loose, didn't fall easy. The lawn where we played was narrow, a few young trees scattered to grow shade and decorate the plot. They didn't get in our way. Half a step clear, I locked my eyes on the pass, opened my arms to a maple I never saw. I couldn't believe the faces I woke to. It was another year. I was a hero. I wanted to keep playing but my head wouldn't rise.

The girl behind me sixth period cried all hour as the radio droned the news of the president's murder. Of course it was a surprise, but more that school was called off, everything closed. We were all learning what to say. When I ran upstairs to tell Mom and Dad the killer was shot, it could've been the weather. Neither one stirred. Then it was spring, and the night he didn't come back. I'd thought of sneaking to the party he said I couldn't go to when he went out for coffee with Mom. The cop behind her at the door with the news was eight feet tall.

The walk to school with the ball wasn't hard, but it was nearly a mile to the lanes after, the thing heavier until I was miserable no matter how many times I changed hands. Still, I always got there. Rick scored much higher, but didn't have his own. I didn't know anyone who did. Too fancy I knew for my low average, and too heavy, but I was going to get stronger, score higher, it'd teach me how. Dad never took me anyway. I had a handicap. Then I tried a lighter one I rented from the lanes. The finger holes fit, my scores went up. We won the championship. It's the only trophy I ever got. It's still in my room.

# COLUMBUS ON HALSTED

THE SPINACH pie's cold, and the young girl is the owner's daughter. She's not pretty. The one who sticks her nose to the glass door is, brown hair falling straight as her eyes, but in a flash she's gone with them. The language inside is foreign.

Two men drink coffee at the next table and the daughter leaves. What else are we here for? Columbus gazes over the floor from the window, right hand spread over the open robe that falls to the end of his skirt. Well dressed and rich, the left rests on a globe. This is the world, and he knows it. Shoulder-length hair, beard and moustache describe the upturned chin. He's Admiral of the Ocean Sea. Plaster noble, he could be Christ, slippered feet posed near right angle in some royal hall. It was never astronomy, math that brought him, but the Bible, dreams, voices. Stories. Pirate, merchant, he'd sailed for years—no one was better at dead reckoning. The men he got from the docks complained and plotted, but he knew the coast was out there. He was crazy.

Property seized from converts and Jews bought the second fleet back. The men he'd left for a colony were killed. He was sure Cuba was mainland. That natives should be slaves or eaten. Then food went bad, and he and his brothers hung the men who crossed them. When the king and queen found out, a new governor came to replace him, sent him back in chains. If only he would speak.

If only we could hear: sure the pie's cold, but it's delicious, coffee fresh and hot. Everyone needs more money, but now Russia's a friend. The faces plodding down the street are tired, the day nearly over. Except it's not; the new shift's coming on. Greek music piped through the ceiling skips and stutters in its track. A black-haired woman comes in and sits with the men. She's never been to France, but her father has, and she loves the language. Two years from Syria, not married, the men can't figure it. Not quite beautiful, but we all watch. The cases around the room brim with sweets. No one comes in to buy. She's a supervisor at the clothes factory down the street, she's going to California, Cancún for vacation. Someone calls to the Mexican busboy: *¿Una bonita chiquita, verdad?* and the kid smiles. She sips coffee the owner brought her, lights a cigarette. Does she like it here? Her smile is faint. If she could get the language, the right man, the leaking apartment roof fixed. She exhales. The cloud scatters before the statue's eyes.

# FIELD BOXES

THERE'S NEW brick parquet, coffee, chairs, music. It's cold, the line's long, but this is an afternoon off, just what we need to remember. I drove fast & early this morning, got to the job on time, and they were glad to see me. The new candidates promise our children will learn to read, we'll be able to pay our bills. The replacement window won't fit, we'll have to do it another way, and it'll cost more. Still, I know how to put in the new trap I got for the drain. The faucet I replaced closes off-center, you have to play with it to find the right angle to shut off the leak, but a little patience and it works. The house isn't falling apart yet. There'll be sweat & beer, green daze & thousands screaming to help us. The pipe smoke in the next aisle smells luscious. I love that red hat, I've never seen anything like it. Breath smoke in the frost, the talk down the row is the country we came for:

"If they'd won just a few of those heartbreakers last year, they'd've been right in it."

We like to be optimistic, but all the money doesn't make them heroes. They're a year older. The next dozen move up, closer to the front.

"No matter what we make in this country, it's too expensive or falls apart."

"All they know how to do is lose," the voice says as it fades, and the conversation's gone.

Then it's my turn. Someone's sweeping the ground around us. The music starts again and we're moving. It's getting exciting, but I'm freezing, and I can't see the end.

# FUSION

THE AFTERNOON Dad took me to the restaurant, we were the only ones there. It was Italian, I must have had some spaghetti, at least a sandwich. His friend's name was Jim. I sat in the green vinyl booth while he went back and talked. It must have been hours. I walked over to the cook's window, but everything was too high to see. I knew better than to complain out loud. We were somewhere in the suburbs. I didn't even bring a book.

Thirty years they've been speeding atoms to break into space, trying to rearrange into heat we can make forever. But the stroller won't go up those stairs. Carry it? Then when the babies get up to the platform, herd them away from the tracks? While I watch the stroller, get 'em all on the train, keep 'em still, then get 'em off downtown and up the subway stairs? Chest tight, scaly patches on elbows, right foot drags its nerve disease. A cab's eight bucks, but still less than a babysitter I can't find anyway. This time I'm going to Mexico. At the fusion conference they laughed at the promise they could hardly measure: "Like a dollar against the national debt. There's no free light."

I could let them run, but the damage is constant. All of us feel the cells piling toward winter. The water off the cliffs at Tulum is so blue I can touch it, feel the long white sand just south where I'll set the tent, gather driftwood, walk the ruins. How long do I have to stay here? When is he coming back?

# BUSINESS ON THE COURSE

THE FIRST SHOT rose perfectly, fell under the hill's crest. When I got there in the cart, the next group was already waiting. We couldn't search forever. I dropped a new one to play where I thought the first had landed, drove it into the woods. Grass thin and dry, a great place to picnic, but who's that screaming on the other side of the fence? The shrieks could be trouble, but with all the kids and noise in these streets, it's almost fun. They say we've got to wipe out those bombs before that country uses them. The last war was such a success, let's do it again. We didn't come to sit around and eat, and we're not staying. I just wanted to enjoy the walk, get some exercise.

Summers after high school I picked up John before light. I couldn't wait to hit the first shot, walk the wet grass, sun just rising. It was called Meadowbrook, though there was no meadow, the brook a swampy creek on the last holes. It was the one game I could win against him, though neither of us were much good. We had a huge breakfast at the end before work. My father loved it, never lost a bet. One birthday he promised to take me, then complained of chest pains, but Mother had him take medicine, and we went. Dead thirty years, I never saw him really play.

Then let's dance. Dick's got a new house to visit, phony wood-grain paneling in the living room, red painted dining room, and it could be twenty years ago. His girlfriend left, but he's having the party anyway. The newest serial killer's safe in jail. Rebels declare cease-fire. One of these people is sure to be the story dying for me to tell on the way to being famous as any.

Last night I never wanted to wake up. News you were sleeping with someone else, kids wheezing their permanent colds, I threw you down the stairs. Good. It's broken. Leave me alone. More information everywhere, but teenage pregnancy rates keep rising. We know the answer is patience. The country we grew up hating on the other side of the world became something else. The woman whose voice breathed into the phone last night said she was sick of teaching history, what can she do with her life? In minutes your old boyfriend's due. At the bar yesterday, you said your body felt so free, arm so light you couldn't bring it down.

I didn't keep track of the score, lost three more balls before I was through. Someone behind us couldn't wait, hit one up and past us. I borrowed a club from your mother and lost it. Bees are everywhere. That woman serves coffee part-time at the café down the block. She made the quiche yesterday, but the peaches are fresh. This trip is only a day, and we can't afford it. I never learned to hit the irons right. When are they going to bring my order?

# PRESIDENTS' DAY

KIDS STOMP through the room "hunting for bear" and
their wooden towers crash. Sun over the carpet, another cup of coffee, we're celebrating heroes. Once
they must have been thoughtless as this play, crops
simply growing in the acres their fathers took from
the wild. These heroes never murdered any natives,
but the savages were such trouble. And the slaves? At
twenty the first inherited eighteen with his land,
owned forty-nine a decade later, though "principled
against this kind of traffic in the human species," he
never sold any. They say he hated the business and
wanted to end it, kept a doctor for them, fed and
dressed and treated them so well that "few" ran away.
He liked to play cards, fish, dance, race horses. He
liked to hunt. Born rich, he got richer. The other was
poor, taught himself, directed the war to keep the
country one though he never fought himself. He
signed the slaves free. His wife went crazy.

If we could only teach them: that castle is great,
why don't you save it? That plug can hurt you, leave it
alone. Those are "bad guys," but it's just tv. Maybe
someone can help. Maybe when you get big, you will.
The new job's supposed to make these days precious,
she'll have dinner ready, and if not we can afford to eat
out. Then a quick drink after work with the woman
who understands these things. Then another. Next
month we'll go to Florida, but those pregnant alcohol-
ics should be put in jail to save their babies' brains. It's
right we have our own house, tropical fruit no matter
the season. The drug dealer ought to be shot. Then

the rapist, ex-con, husband who beats his wife. The balance of payments keeps getting worse, might as well take up smoking again. The FBI's running down the ones who cut electric lines to stop cancer, who ambush machines to save forests. The president smiles and waves. He really does care for us. He tells us every chance we're better off, and he means it. How can we complain? Soon enough those kids tower over us, sweat beer and laugh. Look what I made, one says, this is my gun. His brother says it's beautiful.

# DOUBLE SOLITAIRE

THE WHITE PATCH is barely visible just behind my ring. A half-inch long, forked at the end, two lines crosshatch on the right side of the base of the third finger, close enough to make it a star. No one ever notices. Mary rubs in cream against creases, Bob massages his scalp to bring back hair; but I always wanted to be a pirate: eye patch, scar, war survived for everyone amazed.

Dad gone bowling, dinner and dishes done, homework stacked away, Mom said do we want to play cards?

Yes!

And I'm racing upstairs for the deck in my room. I hardly ever win, especially double solitare—triple tonight, with Barbara—but Mom's fun, even more sometimes with Dad gone, and this game she taught us last week is neat. Baseball records piled on the pine desk in my room, books & notebooks left, and there, the cards: aces for big hits, facecards for singles & walks & errors. Mantle's barely hitting .300, but the season's just started.

At the student teacher's fiesta, I swung blindfolded at the piñata till the bat stopped, Fred Heller moaned and dropped. Last month he'd jumped around so much one day we lost gym. I led the chase after school, caught him by the swamp. I was going to slug him, but he was too big though he hardly fought. I yelled with the other guys behind. He rocked on the tile floor. He didn't come back after lunch.

"How could I see with that blindfold?"

I tried outrage. They couldn't tell even a slit of light. I worked long division till 4 before Mr. Sirotiak let me go home. The time I threw the snowball at Lynn & laughed, she told though it only hit her coat. I said it was someone behind me who threw & ran away, and I just thought it was funny & was pretending so my arm just happened to look like . . .

Now they don't believe anything.

Racing down the hall, gray carpet, black & white & green George & Martha Washington wallpaper blurred, left hand holding the deck exploding against the door frame catching knuckle between two middle fingers. Red dollops track the carpet I cry & stumble downstairs, & Mom'll be mad, I drop to my knees at the bottom, grip my left wrist, blood dripping on shirt, jeans, the tile entryway. I'm trying to keep it off the carpet. I swear I'm trying. Barbara runs to the kitchen, soaks a towel to wrap against the blood.

"Why does this always happen when your father's gone?" Mom says.

*

At the park, in twos and threes, walkers came by with balloons, and our baby toddled at them. Too charmed to say no, the grown-ups gave him one, and he ran off to slide with his treasure.

Then he forgot, let go, watched the balloon fall into the sky & vanish.

When he woke last night and yelled, his whole body shook at the storm. I held him and he stopped. "Wain!" he said. "Lighten! Funda! BangBang!"

Stunned by the flashes in the bathroom window. He stared out as we all sat on the floor. He wanted to go out in it. We watched & talked, then put him back to sleep.

This morning it was all he could say: "Funda! BangBang! Lighten!"

He wanted to know where it was. He put on one of my hats. He wanted to go out and find it. He kept pointing and shouting. He can't imagine what happened. Suddenly there we were.

# SOLO WITH COFFEE

Someone's playing the piano, slow melody improv, high and sweet, and out the window's so bright it's hard to believe how cold. At the nearest table a woman's blond hair shades her eyes, her friend's dark brushes her shoulder amid the conversation—he said yes, last night, that film, or she did—and now every table's filled. For once there's enough money, and it's honky-tonk rag, the room lifts, chili and cheese sandwich in perfect time, newspaper set aside unread. Tonight I'll make that call, get the job done, and the waitress smiles. Is there anything else I want?

Across the country the woman who gave me tea a cloudy afternoon after I'd flown the long day, found the way up to the strange city, who offered me food, room for the night, the soft chair wrapping me still, is dead. I saw her paintings. Clouds gathered and settled down. She meant it when she said I could stay. Of course I couldn't.

Business done, I drove north up the freeway in the dark, found a gas station just in time, but not the latch, or whatever trick to open the tank on the rented car. It wasn't supposed to rain, but it was damp, and I could feel it. And see the night curled up in the back seat under those floodlights, cars a sea lapping by until some cop bangs on the hood, the tow truck comes, no one to answer a late-night call. Funny, if it hadn't been so cold. Then I finally found the button to open the tank and when I got to the house up the coast friends were waiting. We got drunk on Merlot, stood on an empty deck, sky stuffed with stars, night chilled clear.

The piano rag turns soft, falls forward, quickens. Coffee's gone tepid and bitter while I gaze. The man at the next table wants a girlfriend, the one in front borrows a pencil, the waitress tells him she's still seeing that guy but everyone knows it isn't working. That sweater's truly striking. I can feel the swell of her skin. Next to the wall, a child tips over a chair with a bang that turns everyone's head. She doesn't make a sound. The cup's done.

Another? the waitress asks me.

The beautiful women have gone. I don't want anymore.

# TEETH

"WE'VE PLANNED a thousand a month for the house, you'd think we could save," she says, "and it just goes. The rest is the dentist. My bite wore a hole in the bone. For a year every time I smiled there was blood."

She keeps looking over, touching her teeth as she explains. "Two and a half hours, I don't know what they're doing, he's got this assistant. They keep building it up and tearing it down to get it to look right. Two-twenty-five a month, cheap compared to my other dentist. She keeps holding things, handing him something. It's just cosmetic, a subtle thing, you probably don't even notice, but I do. At least now I can look in the mirror."

Blond hair straight over her shoulders, even when she was younger she wasn't pretty enough. I want to touch it. And the other woman's black storm sweeping her face and ears. Then the place is full—someone reading a paper, someone writing, drinking, eating, hum of conversation.

The blonde says she works just enough hours to get the insurance.

"Try it," she says. "Even as a secretary you can work into something creative."

A dental chair? An umbrella?

A hand on her skin. Another glass of wine.

When I look up again, lunch is over.

# WINDOW

ACROSS THE ALLEY, glass frosted so no one can see in.
Nights the light goes on, an arm, silhouette of a body's
statue next to the plant on the sill. A woman? Our
children are practicing words: What that is? they ask
bread, bulldozer, crayon.

The other side of the world celebrates "freedom."
No more meat in those shops than last week, but now
they can talk. Riots in distant cities, grain harvest
down again, the damaged nuclear plant closing. "Divi-
dends" for the end of a war? Words. Tomorrow I'll get
a real job.

A slip of green might be fern, that woman's room.
Tomorrow she'll wave from the window, smile above
the white scrap of cloth draped over the outline of a
breast.

# MANNEQUINS

FROM A DISTANCE, they almost seem beautiful: chocolate, ash, mesquite and white, frozen in the window, clothes draped with such elegance we're supposed to need them. Of course they aren't really women. And we do. The bike in the bedroom corner goes nowhere, but it helps us keep off the weight if we work at it. All weekend we stroll between toys, money, clothes, while the actual women drift off to their country. I know there's a symphony in this town and a museum. We must be lucky. On the coast I just left, the sun shines every day. The riots in China aren't ours. It's raining, and we're here for days. Have a drink for me at that bar, listen to the Dutchman talk. This clothes store has the same name, how could they be related? The only woman in that place was fat and loud as the tv jokes. I couldn't understand half he said, but it sounded exactly right.

# ASTRONOMY

SOME CLOUD'S HIDING cold dark matter, twenty times more than all we can find everywhere, holding the cloud in place. It means the universe is "closed." So Sharon's in Florida, visiting a future: pensioned next to the golf course miles from any waves. This must be the "new." Health costs going up twelve percent. Coach fired. With all his money we can't feel too bad. If I just beat off every day I can forget about sex for hours. The "new reality" those headsets inject might help, but no one wants the lumps in flesh, speed and vertigo piling us into alien slime. All I had to do was clean the wine I spilled on the machine to get it working again, and here we are. True, a few keys stick, but I'm sure we can hum through it.

And if the clouds would actually deliver, or clear, the right one ring the bell, wouldn't we be saved? Well, maybe not you, but me at least. Sharon says she's practicing compliance to bring back. Paul's going south of the border. If I didn't have this cold, I could even laugh. All right, I'll put away the gun for now. The drugs let me sleep, give me something to look forward to: those plants growing on my own acres, ready to cut and sell. Of course it's illegal, but isn't that the interest? They were so visible from every direction, I cut too many down too early. They looked like aspen, or birch, though everyone knew the truth. Paul said there'd still be enough left for a fine crop next year, and he's been in these woods long enough to know. So what if it was a dream? I was young again. Maybe I'm supposed to go on, explain more of the scene, what I was doing there—believe me, I want to. The new alderman ran with a gang. Another family's search ends at the morgue. The sky was pale, light overcast. It was afternoon, any day in spring. There wasn't another sound. The woman going by my table yesterday took my breath away, smiled politely, went on.

# THE NEW JUSTICE

THEY WANT to move the cooler, they're making jokes, they're staring at the wall. They're wedging the plank behind it, but the two-by-ten's not big enough. Still, the repairman thinks the problem is simple. He doesn't see a leak. Clean the coil, let the engine run through the weekend. The band bus is parked outside, all of them gone for supper. There'll be plenty of music later. Didn't the candidate tell the truth? And what about that woman? We all know that flesh can't be trusted. That's why we're here. Every compressor's supposed to have its own circuit, but these old buildings weren't built for the load. Turn off what you don't need, balance what you do. The temperature's falling. I'll drink bourbon. By midnight the room's a howl, someone warns of fire, but it never happens, at least not to anyone we know. Or have I forgotten already? By the time she left for the coast, she couldn't resist him. Storm roared up the chimney, sparks snowing over the rafters. You've got to clean the stack at the beginning of each season; that time we were lucky. Across the world another war is over, but the old city's flattened, and in the capital that used to rule they're combing dumps for clothes. The bartender tosses over a bag of nuts and grins. Oak leaf, trillium, patch of fern in this postcard remind us: we don't live here. The weekend's coming, and we're getting out. How about those stars? Shining through the frame of tree and branch in the picture, there's a line of light: traffic, city, across water or some field. Nothing there sees the camera, or whatever's lighting this scene. The card isn't even signed; just another ad for an exhibit someone wants to be important. The vote goes on, the president's choice installed for life, and whatever we thought was never part of it.

# OUR PARTY

NEW YEAR'S, and a little sleep before our guest threw up at dawn. It was a good party. Sorry I've got to kill something now. Those bodies I saw at the club are exquisite, especially that one, and that one, and— Just another facial tic, mote in the eye I'll get over. No one can resist the funeral, the supermarket, the ball game. When I played guitar at midnight everyone loved it. We had salmon, duck, asparagus with hollandaise, three wines. I could hardly eat. Then I got sick. Okay, so it wasn't her fault. Just keep that gun in the newspaper. Hope the tire won't go flat, or the carburetor explode when the family drives home. These complaints make everyone sick. Temperature slowly rising, enough glass left in the alley for the neighborhood bums to trade for a night's room. Isn't it time you got supper warming? This is the beginning.

*

The walls slid together slowly in the Saturday morning serial I used to watch, the hero due to be crushed. I only smashed three plates this year. "No exit," Bob said we should name the van you want us to take with the kids. You call it vacation. Forget about the story I worked on ten years, it's not going to sell. That prisoner must have been saved, what other point would there be to the show? Helen Sliwa in turn-of-the-century Chicago stockyards had a slaughterer boyfriend, sex with the woman painter. Catchy, but it wasn't my idea. The roofer's coming over to fix the squirrel's damage. And sunshine for no good reason; I don't want to forget that part. My wife got word from the doctor there's a "thing" in her right breast, and she's gone down for him to feel her. All I can do is drive, sing along with the radio, change stations. The news is always murder.

*

Every season infects by surprise, and suddenly we're there. If not predictable in specific, the texture's well known—colors, shapes, particulars glaze over eyes & head reminding that "spiritual" isn't certain knowledge of one thing, but the essential we've got to itemize each day: new light switch in bedroom the wife's been wanting. Space cleared by shelving. Sports on tv. Of course I should be doing the report. Maybe I ought to get stoned and brood. Then her birthday comes again, and the pressure to spend enough on the right thing, as if that'll give us both another year. She wants something personal she can wear—clothes, an ornament singular and elegant, instantly "her." The expensive watch I got her last year was just the thing for that time, but it's lost. This is another year.

# GOD ON KENMORE

YES, HANNAH, of course I'm looking for an answer, and I'd love to hear it from you, the more attractive of the two of you at my door, though you don't say a word after your name is told, young, but not a kid certainly, but not married either. You'd wear a ring, I know, if you were. The brochure in your hand says God, and I surely don't mean to deny Him, or Her, this isn't an excuse. I've had children howling, rash and headache and nowhere, whatever I can't turn from banging every cell. I'm alive. It isn't despair. I know It's not some shirt you outgrow—if She doesn't tatter or get lost first. You might even be interested in that winter night I walked into a billion stars praying. I'm telling you, I was delivered. So why is there sex everywhere, further away? Why do I want a gun?

In the corner of this room, Siva's dancing, twice: the couple's graceful, a red cartoon, as if to remind us how these things must go together. Don't get me wrong, I believe it. The picture was my ex's, mounted for a wall in that house we built. It was the finest house I ever lived in. I could tell you about the red tile trucked all the way from Arizona, laid in concrete and plaster we mixed hot July on the floor in kitchen and bathroom, the yellow pine flooring, the smell of woodsmoke. I could tell you how the scents of pine, the weight of the maul explained everything.

That night wasn't the coldest. She was inside, going through her things, and ours, packing, getting ready to go. I listened for signs, a voice, a hint. An owl knocked back in the woods. There was an engine far away.

Stars were a smear. I knew I was strong. I was going to stay. You could be someone's ex too, your call the answer. Trust me, I'm not making fun. I couldn't stay.

*

D. goes home to blood on the walls. He doesn't know why he called to tell me except that it happened while he was here. A dozen times with a Swiss Army knife & chunks of something, like bottles of ketchup poured everywhere. His friend called emergency, got to the hospital himself. He's not "out of the woods." Barbara stayed a week on our couch, only ate the Christmas present candy, rubbed her face with expensive oil. She knew the clues were in our magazines. She couldn't escape. And disappeared. But he had a good job, worked for the city. Sure the president was after him. His father's a minister, and he's coming. So D.'s cleaning blood off the futon, floor, ceiling, phone, every surface. There's always more.

What happened to silence? Love & bone? Even sex, though the word's already a flag of too much trouble. Look, we don't have to talk about it. The last conversation was downright cheerful—kids drawing and talking about toys, the Florida weather you love so warm. We could have been any friends. Up here, it's almost spring again. But this was supposed to be about God. So here It is, waving all the hands. First the line's busy an hour, then no answer, but It's one way to stand the pain. Try it again. The night's just begun, anything can happen. Then it does.

*

Cheese sandwich at noon. Or dinner with my best friend, either will do. I haven't seen him in years—

brown hair, skin bronze in California sun. He's sitting in a lounge chair left for junk next to a parking lot in this photograph, new book in his lap, both our girlfriends out of sight. I married mine. Then she moved out. At least the rain has stopped. How about that ball team! But that was last year too, and everyone's so busy these days—Renee with her accounts, Gary with his baby . . . The music coming from the ceiling fills the café with religion, dresses the whole street in its robes. Let us pray. I thought that woman was going to kiss me through yesterday's sweat and rain after she found me in her alley. I helped her move out an old couch, rusted cabinets left in her new apartment. Her name was Mary. Of course she didn't. The crowd stringing down the street was evidence the ball game was over. Either side could have won. Nipples stretched against her t-shirt, I couldn't look away. Now it's raining again and I'm late for work. Maybe a cigarette, another drink, things to look foward to overdoing if I can last to the age it won't matter. What was that book? Speak to me. Please.

*

Straw hair, blue sparks as she leans over the table, and I'm listening.

*"It's such a high stress job it's hard to maintain friend-ships."*

Luckily no one's dying, at least that we know. The Baptist who came to our door yesterday said they'd be delighted to send a bus to take us to church. His partner held back, head bent sideways, mouth half-open, astonished stare of alien. Whose planet is it? One more broken door, street racing by while the children upstairs howled after their guns. Let us pray.

The old music in this café croons Kentucky in four parts, Sunday streets deserted; the city must be in church. If only she'd slept with me, if she'd say she wanted to . . . But then she did, and it was another decade. How about that woman there, talking again while she fingers a pearl necklace. Or her. Or her. Experts say breast implants leak ten times more often than companies say. Ten-year-old raped in school. Maybe if I got a tattoo, snakes twisting about my arm to go with this earring. I swear no one notices the stain on the front of this sweater, but my wife says people are just too polite to say. The truckfuls dead and dying are far away. We can forget. We're going next week, for sure.

# PICNIC TABLES

INDIAN PAINTBRUSH, prickly pear cactus yellow flowers budding, a few beautifully open. There's something purple, shades of grass & cactus green to gray, and mountains, snow patched high up to the north, where clouds are settled in, thinning to streaks along ridges & down the long valley south & clear. And light. A horse munching grass just out the door.

And up at the pool, two women blonde & naked. Isn't this why I'm here? I'm building tables, cutting redwood, fitting pieces. I'm only the help. If it doesn't quite work, it's not my job. The point is the view. Another's swimming in the pool, late afternoon, side-stroke one lap, then backstroke, water breaking over breasts, strong arms, legs working. It isn't sex exactly, a lucky thing these days. My own nipples have no more reason than her clitoris's million nerves gathered to pleasure. This is science. This is the cells' incidental work, the animal's million years assembled to the same answer, holding the saw I push along the angle, two planks fifty-nine inches, three at twenty-eight, nine at seventy-one. Then Alan holds when his father takes a turn, the cut binds, snaps back to catch a finger, his face twists near tear.

Dad shakes his head: "You've got to pull it away, like *this*" and the boy walks down the path to take out the splinter, bathe the wound in warm spring, nurse himself.

Or Marty back from divorce, son living with mother in town three hours away, man and woman hating each other too much to talk. He's given up writing

porn, finally back in college studying "land use," on
the way to visit the cabin he built in the mountains.
The dump in the nearest town's got all the newest
technology to get rid of what we can't use. Not perfect, of course, there's still rubber tires, old grease,
pounds not placed where they belong, but they come
for miles to study what's been built, learn how it
works. A half-dozen others built houses up near snow-
line along with Marty. The country's magnificent. Six
months it's snowed in solid. No one can live there.

*

A bird's perched on a woman's finger, a hummingbird
on a branch, and I could listen to this music all day.
The bird's green neon, smuggled from Mexico, and
when I go over, it flitters to my shoulder. Then sleeps.
I want to eat lunch. I want to go back to that pool and
swim while the sun's still out. The woman who
brought the bird reaches out, takes it back. I want to
build the rest of those tables.

ABOUT THE BOOK

This book was designed by Allan Kornblum, and was set in Dante and Albertus typefaces. It has been printed on acid-free paper, and smyth sewn for reading comfort and added durability. It has been printed and bound at Friesen Printers.